Black Boy Be You!

By Latoshia Martin

Illustrated by Abira Das

BLACK BOY BE YOU

BLACK BOY BE YOU © 2020 Latoshia Martin

All rights reserved. This book or parts thereof may not be reproduced in any form, stored in a retrieval system, or transmitted in any form by any means—electronic, mechanical, photocopy, recording, or otherwise—without prior written permission of the publisher, except as provided by the United States of America copyright law.

ISBN: 9798677846243

Printed in the United States of America
First Edition: September 2020
Illustrations : Abira Das

Dedicated to my supportive husband who allows me to shine.

This book is for my two handsome sons that inspired me to write this book.

Isaiah got up early ready for the day.

"I am ready for the park," Isaiah yells to his mom as he puts on his shoes.

Every Saturday Isaiah and his mom walk to the park.

"Park day, park day, I love park day,"
Isaiah sings as he bounces down the street.

"I see my friends mom," he yells as he runs to the slide.

"Why?" asked Isaiah

" Different? Different?," Isaiah repeated out loud. "What makes me different ?," he ask himself.

My nose is a little bit wider and my lips are bigger than my friends.

I wear my hair differently than my friends.

But.... that's okay
Black boy be you!

My skin is darker than some of my friends.

But.... that's okay
Black boy be you!

"I am different and that's okay," Isaiah says proudly.

Black boy be you!

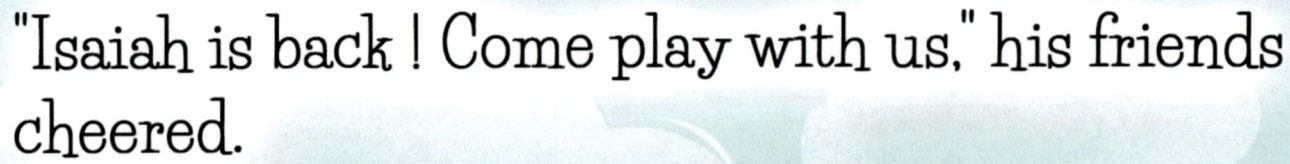

"Isaiah is back! Come play with us," his friends cheered.

"Time to go," Isaiah's mom shouts.

"Go wash up for lunch," his mom tells him.

I do look different from my friends.
But .... I love my nose, my hair, and my skin!

Black Boy Be You!

Made in the USA
Monee, IL
01 January 2021